For Rufus ♥

First published 2005 by Walker Books Ltd
87 Vauxhall Walk, London SE11 5HJ

2 4 6 8 10 9 7 5 3 1

© 2005 Lucy Cousins

The author/illustrator has asserted her moral rights

This book was handlettered by Lucy Cousins

Printed in China

British Library Cataloguing in Publication Data:
a catalogue record for this book is available from the British Library

ISBN 1-84428-022-5

www.walkerbooks.co.uk

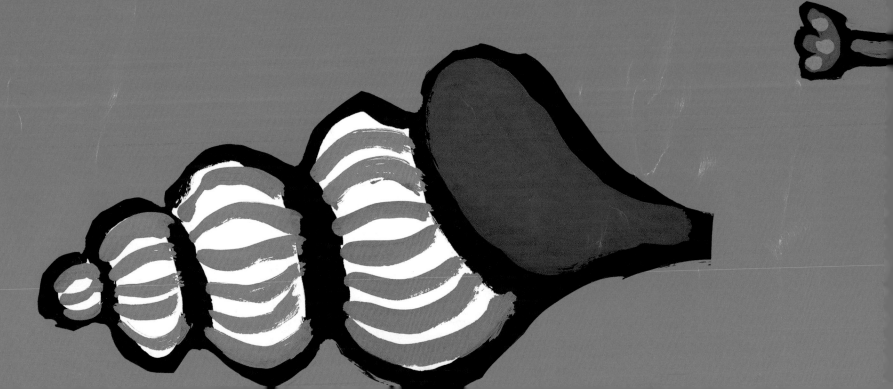

Hooray for Fish!

Lucy Cousins

WALKER BOOKS
AND SUBSIDIARIES
LONDON · BOSTON · SYDNEY · AUCKLAND

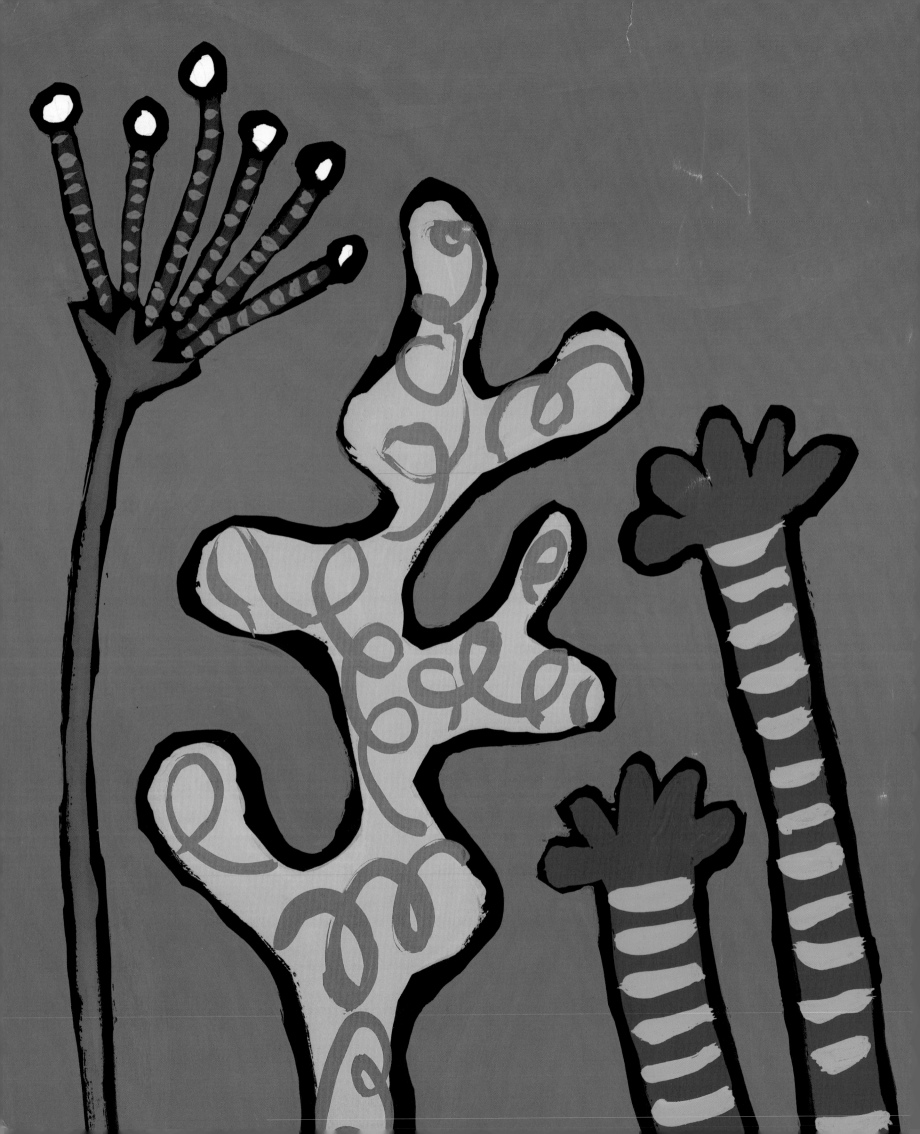

Hello! I am Little Fish,
swimming in the sea.
I have lots of fishy friends.
Come along with
me.

Hello, hello, hello, fish,

red,
blue

and yellow fish.

Hello, spotty fish,

stripy fish,

happy fish,

grumpy fish.

One,
two,
three...

22222 2

3333 333

How many can you see?

Hello, ele-fish,

shelly
fish.

Hello,
hairy fish,

scary fish,

eye fish,

shy fish,

Hello,
fat and
thin fish.

Hello, twin

fin-fin fish.

Curly Whirly,

twisty twirly,

upside
down,

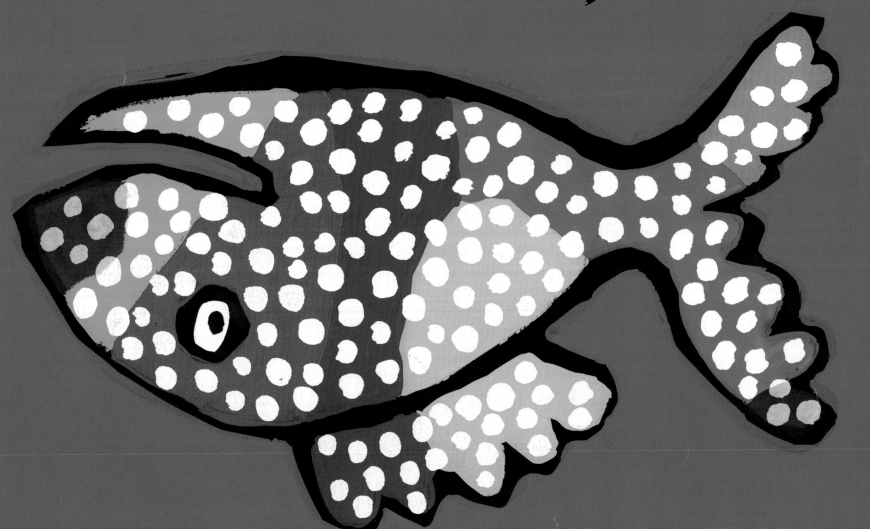

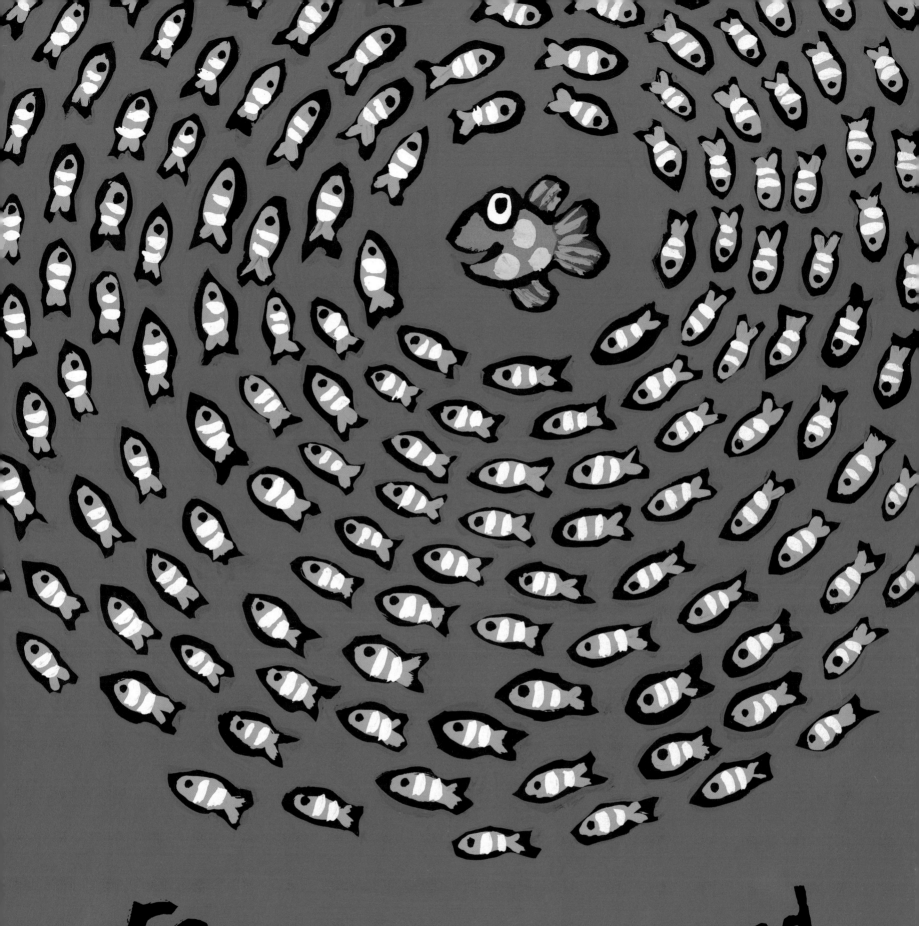

round and round.

So many friends,

so many fish,

splosh, splash, splish!

But where's the one
I love the best,
even more
than all the rest?

Hello, Mum.
Hello, Little
Fish.

Kiss, kiss, kiss, Hooray for fish!